What is a Polydactyl Cat?

J. Antoinette

For Nellie and Ernie. ♥

What is a Polydactyl Cat?

J. Antoinette

I am a polydactyl cat.

What exactly is a polydactyl cat?

Is it a cat soaring
through the skies with
pterodactyls, high above
the rustling trees?

Or perhaps a cat with webbed feet, equipped to dive into the depths of the vast seas?

Could a polydactyl cat magically turn purple with pink polka dots?

Is it a frog-like feline that feasts on flies

and lively hops?

Or maybe...

It means I have

THUMBS!

I have extra digits, thumb-like appendages that make my paws look like mittens.

I've had them since I was just a kitten.

Some people believe
polydactyl cats are lucky.

My wider paws make me a stronger predator,

while still remaining as benevolent as Ernest Hemingway's trusted editor.

I can gracefully
maneuver and climb,
using my agile thumbs
to maintain perfect
balance.

However, my
extraordinary thumbs
come with other
unusual talents.

I can create hand turkeys with you on Thanksgiving

and unlatch doors to join you for comforting cuddles while you're sleeping.

But above all else, my additional beans help me grip my mom's hand tighter,

ensuring she always knows-

I love her from the tip of my head to the touch of my extra toes.

Polydactyl cats are born with a genetic mutation that causes extra thumb-like appendages on one or more paws. But don't worry; these kitty thumbs are harmless to cats. In fact, most cats use the extra toes to their advantage when climbing or hunting.

You may have heard polydactyl cats referred to as Hemingway cats. That's because Ernest Hemingway, a renowned American writer and author of adventurous life and literary works such as "The Old Man and the Sea," housed many of these cats at his home. Hemingway's tale of feline companionship began with Snow White, an all-white polydactyl cat gifted to him by a sea captain in the 1930s. At the time, sailors believed that these cats brought good luck because they helped catch mice on board the ships. When Hemingway learned about these special cats, his love for them grew, and soon he was housing up to 200 of them. To this day, many of Snow White's descendants roam Hemingway's home and can still be visited at the Ernest Hemingway Home and Museum in Key West, Florida.

Polydactyl cats, with their fascinating extra toes, showcase the wonders of nature's genetic diversity. So, the next time you come across a polydactyl cat, appreciate their remarkable thumbs and remember the captivating tale they share with a literary legend. These enchanting creatures serve as a testament to the beauty of diversity and the enduring impact that a furry companion can have on our lives.